The Usborne
Big Book
of
Animals

Illustrated by Fabiano Fiorin
Written by Hazel Maskell

Designed by Stephen Wright

Animal experts: Dr. John Rostron
and Dr. Margaret Rostron

Edited by Alex Frith

Usborne Quicklinks

For links to websites where you can watch video clips of animals
and find lots of animal facts, go to the Usborne Quicklinks website
at **www.usborne.com/quicklinks** and type in the title of this book.
Please follow the internet safety guidelines at
the Usborne Quicklinks website.

How big is BIG?

Some animals are very TALL. Some are very LONG. Others are very HEAVY.

Elephants are the heaviest land animals. Some weigh more than 70 people put together.

Elephant tusks are very long teeth.

Turn the page to see the BIGGEST animal of all...

Giraffes are the tallest animals. The biggest grow over 5m (16 feet) tall – that's taller than a double-decker bus.

A giraffe's neck alone is as tall as a person.

Some **reticulated pythons** grow 10m (33 feet) long – about as long as a bus.

Mice grow to around 10cm (4 inches) long.

A python squeezes its prey to death with its long, muscular body.

A big mouse's body is about this long.

10cm (4 inches)

The biggest animal of all

The blue whale is the biggest animal that has ever lived – even bigger than the biggest dinosaur.

The largest blue whales weigh more than a medium-sized plane, and are over 30m (100 feet) long – longer than a tennis court.

A blue whale's tongue alone is as heavy as an elephant.

Whales come up to the surface to breathe air, through these breathing holes.

The biggest whales eat tiny living things that float in the water. Sometimes, the amount they eat in a day adds up to the weight of a hippopotamus.

Its mouth can hold enough water to fill 400 bathtubs.

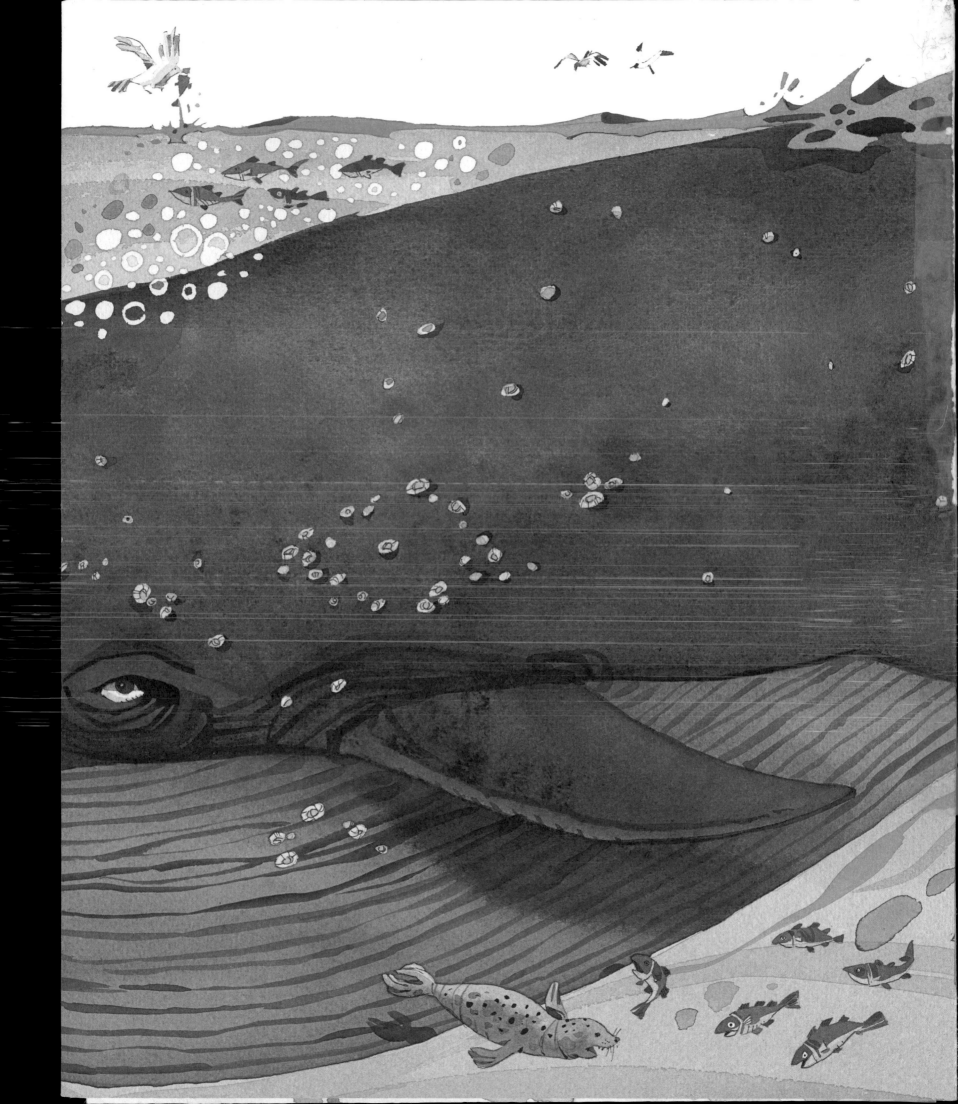

Big birds

Most birds are little and light – it helps them take off and fly. But some are big, and some are even too big to fly.

Pelicans have big beaks that can hold dozens of fish at a time.

Ospreys pluck fish out of the water with their powerful feet.

The tallest **flamingoes** have legs that are over 1m (3 feet) long – longer than the rest of their bodies.

Wandering albatrosses have the widest wings of any bird.

Each albatross wing is as wide as a person with their arms stretched out.

Cranes are the tallest flying birds. Some can grow nearly 2m (6 feet) high – that's as tall as a man.

Lammergeiers often eat bones. They drop bigger bones onto rocks, to shatter them into smaller bite-sized pieces.

Dangerous animals

Most of these animals are fierce hunters, but three of the biggest – hippos, buffalo and rhinos – only eat plants. But they're so big they can easily trample on other animals.

Hippopotamus
Length: some are over 3m (10 feet) long
Weight: some are over 3,600 kg (8,000lbs)
Hippos spend up to 16 hours a day wallowing in water.

Hyena
Shoulder height: up to 90cm (3 feet)
Weight: up to 85kg (190lbs)
Hyenas aren't cats or dogs. Their closest relatives are small animals called civets.

Jaguar
Length: up to 2m (6 feet)
Weight: up to 160kg (350lbs)
Jaguars have the strongest bite of any cat.

Lion
Length: some are over 2m (6 feet) long
Weight: up to 250kg (550lbs)
Lions are the only cats that live and hunt in groups.

Black bear

Grizzly (brown) bear

Bear
Shoulder height: often over 1m (3 feet)
Weight: up to 1,000kg (2,200lbs)
Grizzly bears and polar bears are the largest animals that hunt on land.

Komodo dragon
Length: some are over 3m (10 feet) long
Weight: up to 160kg (350lbs)
Komodo dragons are the biggest lizards.

African buffalo

Length: some are over 3m (10 feet) long
Widest horn span: over 1m (3 feet)
African buffalo live in herds
of up to 2,000.

Rhinoceros

Length: up to 4m (13 feet)
Rhinos are the second biggest
land animals, *after* elephants.

Tiger

Length: up to 3m (10 feet)
Weight: up to 300kg (660lbs)
Tigers are the longest,
heaviest cats of all.

Leopard

Length: up to 2m (6 feet)
Weight: up to 90kg (200lbs)
Most leopards are yellow
with black spots, but some
are black all over.

Puma

Length: up to 2m (6 feet)
Weight: up to 120kg (260lbs)
Pumas can leap over five times
their height up off the ground.

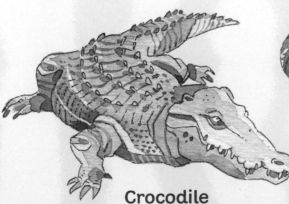

Crocodile

Length: up to 7m (23 feet)
Weight: up to 1,000kg (2,200lbs)
Some crocodiles have as
many as 70 teeth.

King cobra

Length: up to 5m (16 feet)
Height: they can rear up
over 1m (3 feet)
King cobras are the biggest
poisonous snakes.

Anaconda

Length: up to 10m (33 feet)
Weight: up to 250kg (550lbs)
Anacondas are the heaviest snakes.

Creepy crawlies

These creepy crawlies are all about the same size as they are in real life.

Creepy crawlies are often small and hide away.
But some grow so big you can't miss them...

Bumblebee

Big **goliath beetles** are as large as a big mouse.

Big **stick insects** can stretch out longer than an adult's hand and forearm.

Goliath birdeaters are the biggest spiders. They are so big they can eat bats and lizards – but they don't actually eat birds.

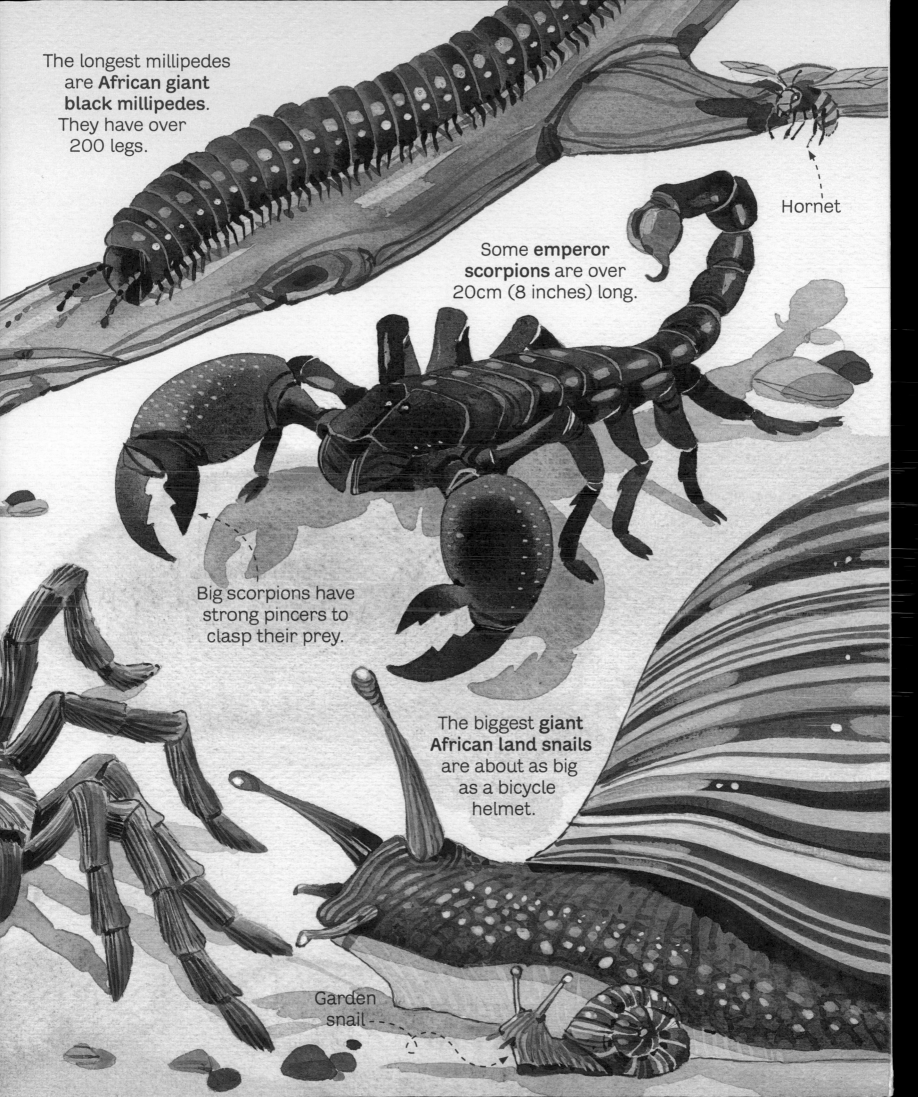

The longest millipedes are **African giant black millipedes**. They have over 200 legs.

Hornet

Some **emperor scorpions** are over 20cm (8 inches) long.

Big scorpions have strong pincers to clasp their prey.

The biggest **giant African land snails** are about as big as a bicycle helmet.

Garden snail

Polar animals

Big animals live all around the world – even in the freezing lands and oceans around the North and South Poles.*

Lynx

Length: over 1m (3 feet)
Weight: up to 40kg (90lbs)
Lynxes can hunt animals more than three times heavier than they are.

Moose

Length: some are over 3m (10 feet) long
Shoulder height: up to 2m (6 feet)
Moose are the biggest deer of all.

Polar bear

Length: up to nearly 3m (10 feet)
Weight: up to 680kg (1,500lbs)
A polar bear's top swimming speed is 10kph (6mph).

Antarctic fur seal

Length: up to 2m (6 feet)
Weight: up to 210kg (460lbs)
Males have a long mane, with thick fat and muscles underneath.

Leopard seal

Length: some are over 3m (10 feet) long
Weight: up to 460kg (1,000lbs)
Of all seals, leopard seals are the fiercest hunters. Some even hunt other seals.

Walrus

Length: some are over 3m (10 feet) long
Weight: up to 2,000kg (4,400lbs)
Walruses are much bigger than all seals, except elephant seals.

* The symbol by each animal shows whether it lives in the North or the South.

Emperor penguin – the biggest kind

Adélie penguin

Penguin
Height: some are over 1m (3 feet) tall
Weight: up to 40kg (90lbs)
Penguins can go 20 minutes without breathing – longer than any other bird.

Reindeer
Shoulder height: the tallest are over 1m (3 feet) tall
Reindeer travel up to 5,000km (3,100 miles) each year to find food.

Wolf
Length: over 1m (3 feet) long
Top speed: up to 65kph (40mph)
Wolves can hear other packs' howls from 10km (6 miles) away.

A male hooded seal blows air into red skin on his nose when he's looking for a mate.

Weddell seal
Length: up to 3m (10 feet)
Weight: up to 600kg (1,300lbs)
Weddell seals live the furthest south of any seals.

Muskox
Length: over 2m (6 feet)
Weight: up to 400kg (880lbs)
Muskox hair grows up to 60cm (2 feet) long – among the longest of any animal.

Hooded seal
Length: over 2m (6 feet)
Weight: up to 410kg (900lbs)

Only male narwhals have tusks.

Narwhal
Length: up to 8m (26 feet)
Tusk length: up to almost 3m (10 feet) long
Narwhals can dive nearly 2km (over 1 mile) down to find food.

Southern elephant seal
Length: up to 6m (20 feet)
Weight: up to 5,000kg (11,000lbs)
Southern elephant seals are the biggest, heaviest seals of all.

Sea creatures

Seas and oceans are home to many of the biggest creatures of all. With water to support their weight, sea creatures can grow to massive sizes.

Whale sharks are the biggest fish. Some are over 12m (40 feet) long – that's as long as a bus.

The biggest **octopus** arms are longer than a broom handle.

Each arm has two rows of suction pads.

This razor-sharp tooth is longer than your thumb.

Some whale sharks' mouths are wider than a doorway – but they only eat tiny things floating in the water.

The biggest **tuna** are longer and heavier than a horse.

Great white sharks are the biggest fish that hunt other animals.

Large **manta rays** weigh as much as a car, but they move gracefully by flapping their wing-like fins.

What's hiding here? Turn the page to find out...

Biggest, fastest, heaviest...

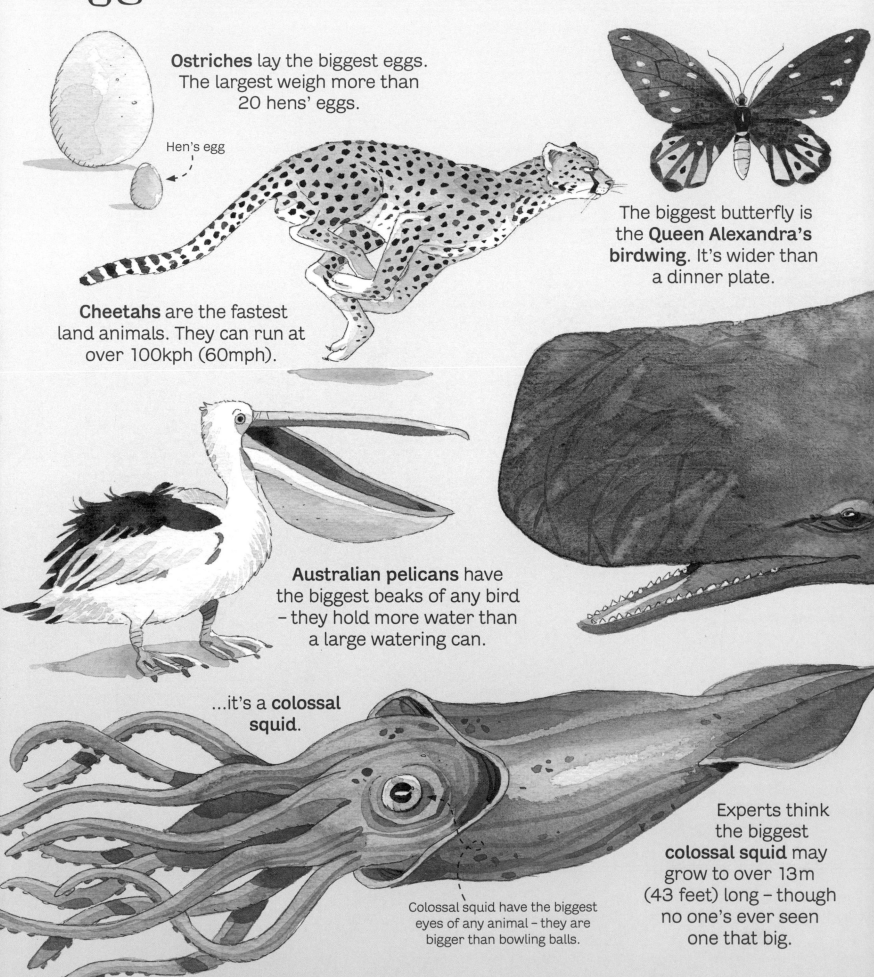

Ostriches lay the biggest eggs. The largest weigh more than 20 hens' eggs.

Hen's egg

Cheetahs are the fastest land animals. They can run at over 100kph (60mph).

The biggest butterfly is the **Queen Alexandra's birdwing**. It's wider than a dinner plate.

Australian pelicans have the biggest beaks of any bird – they hold more water than a large watering can.

...it's a **colossal squid**.

Colossal squid have the biggest eyes of any animal – they are bigger than bowling balls.

Experts think the biggest **colossal squid** may grow to over 13m (43 feet) long – though no one's ever seen one that big.

This bird weighs about as much as a 4-year-old child.

The heaviest flying bird is the **great bustard**.

The tallest dog is the **Great Dane**.

The biggest Great Danes are as tall as a Shetland pony.

A chihuahua is about as tall as a can of beans.

The biggest hunter is the **sperm whale**. It grows much longer than a bus, and hunts huge animals including colossal squid.

Series designer: Mary Cartwright   Series editor: Jane Chisholm
Additional design: Lisa Verrall   Digital manipulation: John Russell

This edition first published in 2017 by Usborne Publishing Ltd., Usborne House, 83-85 Saffron Hill, London EC1N 8RT, England. www.usborne.com